THE
DEX-TERMINATOR

Don't miss these other Dexter adventures available in a store near you!

chapter books

#1 Dexter's Ink
#2 The Dex-Terminator

picture books

Horse of a Different Dexter

THE
DEX-TERMINATOR

BY
bobbi JG weiss and
David cody weiss

based on
"DExTER'S Laboratory,"
as created by
Genndy Tartakovsky

SCHOLASTIC INC.

New York   Toronto   London   Auckland   Sydney
Mexico City   New Delhi   Hong Kong   Buenos Aires

ISBN 0-439-38580-6

Cover and interior illustrations by John Kurtz
Designed by Maria Stasavage

12 11 10 9 8 7 6 5 4 3 2 1   2 3 4 5 6 7/0

Printed in the U.S.A.
First Scholastic printing, June 2002

special thanks to veronica ambrose, allison kaplinsky, annie liebert, sophia psomiadis, and maria stasavage for making this book possible.

THE
DEX-TERMINATOR

Chapter 1

"PASSWORD, PLEASE."

"Black hole."

"THAT IS CORRECT."

Dexter hummed happily to himself as the bookcase in his bedroom slid up to reveal a secret room behind the wall. Dexter stepped into his secret laboratory, the world of his dreams. "Saturday at last."

He sighed. "Nothing lies before me but a glorious day of uninterrupted Science!"

Dexter's lab was the place where his genius ideas became reality. Rubbing his hands in anticipation, Dexter strode to his central computer console. "Computer," he said, "display current schedule of experiments, please."

Strangely, the computer didn't respond. No lights flashed upon its vast control panel. No comforting clicks or clacks issued from its speakers. The enormous screen remained blank.

Dexter blinked. "Computer?"

Still no response. It had spoken to him just moments before. It had opened his secret lab entrance and transported him down. But now — nothing.

Dexter's heart skipped a beat. Could it be true? Could his beloved Computer be *broken*??

"Okay, Dexter, remain calm," he told himself sternly. "Surely it is just a minor malfunction that requires the smallest of adjustments." He fiddled with a few controls and stepped back. "That should do it. Computer?"

Nothing.

Near panic, Dexter hurried to open the access panel. He spent the next hour going over every microcircuit, every chip, every inch of Computer's

Motherboard. Still the machine did not respond.

"Noooooo!" Dexter cried, flinging himself across the keyboard. "It cannot be! Oh, my darling Computer, you are too young to die!"

That's when he saw it. Sprawled on the console, Dexter had a perfect view of the narrow space behind Computer. There lay its main power cable — chewed in half.

"Well, no wonder," Dexter said to himself in relief. "Of course, Computer cannot work if the power cable is chewed in half."

He paused. *Chewed in half?*

Alarmed, Dexter grabbed the cable and examined it. Sure enough, it was in two pieces, frayed at both ends. And there were *teeth* marks on it.

Dexter scratched his head, puzzled. What could have possibly caused such damage? The family dog had a habit of chewing the pillows on the living room couch, but Dexter didn't allow him inside his lab. Dexter's sister, Dee Dee, managed to sneak into his lab all too often, but she confined her mischief to pushing

buttons, not chewing cables. So what could it be?

Dexter glanced up, wondering, and was shocked at the sight that met his eyes. He'd been so focused on fixing Computer that he'd ignored the rest of his lab. Now he saw that it was in shambles. There were little teeth marks on *all* his machines. The power cables that criss-crossed the lab were sending sparks into the air. Broken wires and antennas from his inventions littered the floor. Smoke rose from damaged machinery. Beakers lay smashed on the floor, with blue, red, and green liquids oozing from them. Even his work chair had been ripped up. It had gobs of stuffing sticking out of it.

Dexter took one look at the damage,

and a terrible thought popped into his head. "No!" he cried in alarm, and raced to another section of

his lab. It was just as he'd dreaded. There was a small cage on a pedestal, and its door was *open.*

"Ro-Dent!" Dexter said in dismay. "He is loose!"

Exactly one week ago, Dexter had come up with the idea for Ro-Dent, the world's first organic Dust Muncher. It had all started when he saw his mother trying to vacuum behind the sofa. She was complaining, "Dust, everywhere dust! If only

there was some way to keep dust from collecting in corners I can't reach!"

It was then the inspiration for his latest brilliant invention had struck. Dexter had decided to transform a typical white lab mouse into a robotic dust-eating machine. His lab had never been cleaned by his mother, or him, and it was covered with dust. Once his invention was complete, he would then let the mouse free in the lab and it would happily eat all those annoying balls of dust that were impossible to reach. "Science is a wonderful thing," he'd reflected proudly.

But now, somehow, Ro-Dent had got-

ten free — before he'd been properly programmed to eat dust. So far, Dexter had only managed to turbocharge the mouse's metabolism, supplement his strength, and amplify his appetite. "If I don't catch my creation soon," Dexter muttered, "he will devour my entire laboratory!"

He crept around, looking for the mouse, peeking under tables, poking behind machines, and opening all his tool drawers. But there was no sign of Ro-Dent.

Finally, Dexter spotted the mouse on the far side of the lab. Ro-Dent was just

a tiny white spot in the shadows between two generators — and he was chewing on yet another power cable!

Munch. Munch. Munch.

"YOU!" Dexter howled. "You cable-crunching criminal! You knob-nibbling nuisance! You insulation-ingesting interloper!" Dexter grabbed a broom and charged. "Stop eating my laboratory!"

Ro-Dent looked up just in time to see his creator bearing down on him. His little mouse eyes bugged out, and he squeaked in alarm. And then Dexter was upon him and —

— the broom went *THWAK!*

Chapter 2

"Drat," Dexter grumbled. "I missed."

Ro-Dent raced away, zigging and zagging through Dexter's lab like a little streak of lightning. Dexter took off after him, thumping at the mouse over and over again. He missed every time.

Panting for breath, Dexter finally gave up. This was no way to solve the problem. "For the love of Einstein, I am a boy ge-

nius, not a janitor with bad aim," he declared, tossing the broom aside. "The solution lies in *Science*!"

* * * * *

An hour later, Dexter carefully placed a small orange ball on the floor in what he calculated to be the exact center of his laboratory. "This Cheese Bomb should solve the problem," he murmured, pleased with himself. "Never underestimate the power of cheddar!"

With the Cheese Bomb in place, Dexter tiptoed behind a file cabinet and pulled out his remote control. "Oh, Ro-Dent!" he called in a high-pitched singsong, his finger poised over the ACTIVATE button. "I

have brought a yummy, cheesy snack for you!"

Ro-Dent poked his head out from behind the huge fins of a half-built rocket ship. His little black nose twitched with interest. Dexter watched as slowly, tentatively, the mouse crept up to the Cheese Bomb. Ro-Dent sniffed at it, then opened his mouth. Dexter's finger tensed. Ro-Dent took a nibble. Dexter hit the button.

Ka-BLAM! The Cheese Bomb exploded into a gooey orange mess.

Dexter leaped out of hiding and rushed to retrieve Ro-Dent. The mouse was sure to be stuck in the gooey cheddar. But when he reached the center of the lab, there was no sign of the mouse. "What?" Dexter cried, examining the cheddar

trap. It was only too plain. There was a small, round hole in the cheddar goo, surrounded by lots of tiny teeth marks. Ro-Dent had been captured as planned, but he had eaten his way free in only a few seconds.

Dexter frowned, then gritted his teeth. "Very well. I must devise a more devious plan!"

* * * * *

Dexter hung like a silent mini-helicopter twenty feet above the laboratory floor. His Hover-Pack was one of his favorite inventions, and it certainly came in handy now.

Dexter gave a test pull on the string in his hand. It was attached to the door of a wire cage on the floor below. As he

pulled, the cage's door slid up and open.
He eyed the pile of food inside the cage.
"I shall utilize a simple, elegant, time-
honored solution," he said to himself.
Then he called out softly, "Oh, Ro-Dent!
Dinnertime!"

As if on cue, Ro-Dent instantly ap-

peared below. The mouse approached the cage, sniffing eagerly. He stopped at the door and looked around, but saw no sign of Dexter. The boy genius stifled a chuckle as Ro-Dent entered the cage and began eating.

Everything was going exactly as he'd planned! Dexter let go of the string, and the cage door fell shut.

"I have you now!" Dexter cried, zooming down to ground level to retrieve his prize. But as his feet touched the floor, he saw a blur of silver inside the cage. With a squeak of triumph, Ro-Dent burst free and scurried away.

Dexter's mouth fell open. In less than four seconds, Ro-Dent had *eaten* a hole through *metal wire*! "Holy Newton's

autoclaves, I did not realize just how much I increased his appetite," Dexter muttered. "This calls for drastic measures!"

* * * * *

Motors hummed. Servers whined. Dexter made the final adjustments to the huge Robo-Suit he was wearing.

He was ready.

"Beware, Ro-Dent," he said, clomping across the lab with heavy robot steps.

"I will get you now!"

He spotted the mouse ahead, gnawing on the leg of a chair. As soon as Ro-Dent saw the enor-

mous mechanical thing coming for him, he let out a squeak of fear and took off at light speed. Dexter followed, the ground shaking under his great metal feet as he thundered along.

He cornered Ro-Dent and extended his turbo-hand. "Now you are mine!" Dexter cried gleefully. He clenched his fist, triggering his glove mechanism. A Non-Destructo Fiber-Cage propelled by four tiny rockets shot out toward Ro-Dent. The mouse tried to flee, but the cage followed his every move like a heat-seeking missile. At last, with a squeak of dismay, Ro-Dent tumbled across the floor.

The manic mouse tried to nibble his way free, but he couldn't break the Non-Destructo Fiber. He was trapped at last.

18

Chapter 3

Dexter couldn't help but grin. Ah, sweet success! What a wonderful sensation. He never got tired of it.

He was busy working on his next invention when Dee Dee danced into the lab. "Whatcha doin', Dex?" she asked, twirling and leaping into the air.

Dexter tried to ignore her. But Dee Dee wasn't easy to ignore.

"Ooo, what's that?" she asked, sticking her head right between Dexter and the gadget he was adjusting. Unfortunately, that meant that he could no longer see what he was doing.

"I am constructing a Non-Destructo Fiber enclosure," Dexter replied, pushing her head out of the way.

"Ooo," said Dee Dee. She paused. "What for?"

Dexter pointed at the small bundle on the table. It was Ro-Dent, still trapped in the cage.

Dee Dee took one look at the mouse and whirled on Dexter angrily. "You've

got a poor little helpless mousie all tied up!" she cried.

"Helpless, my sweet pajamas — !" Dexter retorted, but before he could finish, Dee Dee had snatched up Ro-Dent. With a flick of her wrist, she'd freed him.

Squeaking in triumph, Ro-Dent leaped off the worktable and dashed into the shadows.

Dexter jumped up and down in fury. "Dee Dee, do you know what you have just done?!"

"Yes!" Dee Dee cheered. "I've freed a cuddly little mousie."

"No!" Dexter howled in frustration. "Oh, you are stuuuupid, do you hear me? Stuuuuupid!"

"Oh, yeah?" said Dee Dee. "Well, if I'm stuuuuupid, you're mean!"

"I am not mean!" Dexter said. With a sigh, he explained it all to her — his experiments on Ro-Dent, and how the mouse was conditioned to eat anything and everything. "I was going to complete my experiment and program his appetite for dust, but noooooo!" Dexter finished.

"*You* had to interfere and now that eating machine will devour my laboratory!"

Dee Dee cocked her head, tongue out, thinking hard. "Oops," she said at last.

"Oops?" cried Dexter. "Is that all you have to say? *Oops?!*"

"No, dear brother," said Dee Dee. "Then I'll help!"

Dexter paused a moment, then shook his head. "No."

"Yes!"

"No!"

"Yes!"

"No!"

"Please?"

"Fine." Dexter slumped.

Dee Dee smiled and grabbed a bottle

of glue from Dexter's worktable. Before her brother could utter a word, she squirted it all over the floor.

"Aaaaaagh!" Dexter shrieked. "Dee Dee, what are you doing?!"

"All we have to do is chase Ro-Dent down this way, and he'll get stuck in the glue," Dee Dee replied reasonably.

Dexter sighed. It was worth a try.

Using a Pest Detector he'd invented, Dexter located Ro-Dent behind a stack of astronomy books. With Dee Dee's help, he flushed the mouse out of hiding and herded him toward the glue floor. But as they approached it, Dee Dee executed a particularly high leap over the glue and, in the process, knocked Dexter into it. He fell face-first into the gloppy mess as Ro-

Dent, giving a little mouse giggle, scampered away.

"Oops," said Dee Dee. She had to stifle a giggle herself.

Dexter sat up and tried to wipe his face. His hands stuck to his cheeks. "Dee Dee," he said, moments before his mouth set into a stiff glue frown. "Please, no more 'Oops'!"

Dee Dee pirouetted through the lab, a box of Whisker-Lickin' Mousie Treats in her hands. As she danced, she placed treat after treat on the floor, form-ing a long, neat line of mousie snacks. The line led to a pile of treats on a spot marked with an **X**. "This will work, Dexter," she assured her brother. "Trust me. Mousie Treats are like candy to mice, and *everybody* likes candy, right?"

"You are the expert," Dexter grum-

bled. He was fiddling with a complex-looking machine that had a big swivel arm. A ray gun was attached to one end of the arm. Dexter checked it carefully, then turned to Dee Dee. "If Ro-Dent takes the bait," he said, "he will end up sitting on that **X**. At that moment, my Molecular Transpositionator will instantly transport him back into his cage."

"Like I said," Dee Dee said proudly, "a perfect plan."

With his adjustments finished and the treats ready, Dexter and Dee Dee hid behind a table. Almost immediately, Ro-Dent appeared and began to eat the line of Mousie Treats. He inched closer and closer to the **X** until finally, he was squatting right on top of it.

Dexter gripped the remote control in his hand. "Perfect," he whispered to his sister. "Now to press the button —"

"Let me do it," Dee Dee whispered back, and she grabbed the remote control. "This big red one, right?" she asked, push-ing it.

"Noooooo," Dexter yelled, "the *blue* one!"

Too late. The tar-geting mechanism of the Molecular Transpositionator shifted, and the bulky ray gun swiveled around — right at Dexter. "Ulp!" was all he had time to gasp before he was zapped by a

bright yellow ray. The next thing he knew, he was squashed inside Ro-Dent's tiny cage.

"Dexter!" called Dee Dee. "Oh, Dexter, where did you go?"

"I've been transported into Ro-Dent's cage by mistake!" Dexter answered, but what actually came out was, *"Hmff mffgh cgrbll bft grrrrph!"*

"Oh, Dexter, where are you?" Dee Dee sang out again. "Yoo-hoo, Dexter!"

"Mm rttth hhrrr!" Dexter said.

At last Dee Dee found him stuffed in the tiny cage. She regarded him thoughtfully. "Don't worry, Dexter, I have an idea. Be right back!" And she danced away.

"Gtt mmm owwwt!" Dexter yelled, but she was gone.

* * * * *

An hour later, Dexter managed to free himself by unhooking the cage latch with the toe of his boot — the only part of his body he could manage to poke through

the wires. He felt like he'd shrunk a few inches, but at least he could breathe again.

When Dee Dee returned, he was ready to kick her right back out of the lab. But she was carrying a scruffy tabby cat. "Meet Bruiser," she said to Dexter. "He's a guaranteed mouser. If you want to catch a mouse, why not use a kitty cat?" She nuzzled Bruiser, who purred back. "Oooo, and he's soooo cute!"

Dexter frowned. "Dee Dee, that is a living, breathing feline. There are no ON or OFF buttons. There is no control device. How can I make him do what I want?"

"Trust in instinct, little brother. Go on, Bruiser," she said, putting the cat down. "Go get the mouse!"

Bruiser began to explore the lab, his nose sniffing. A few moments later, Dexter heard a startled mouse squeak. Then he heard a rather vicious mouse squeak. Next he heard a cat howl. And then Bruiser came tearing back out of the lab, looking scared out of his wits. He leaped at Dexter and clawed Dexter's face in terror before fleeing back upstairs.

Dexter whirled on Dee Dee. "I have no more time for your fooooolishness!" he yelled angrily. "With each passing hour, Ro-Dent's appetite grows bigger! If I do not catch him soon, he will —"

"— eat his way out of the lab?" Dee Dee said, glancing up.

Dexter followed his sister's gaze, just in time to see Ro-Dent disappear up through a hole he'd chewed in the ceiling.

Oops.

Chapter 4

Dexter and Dee Dee raced out of the lab and into the house. Ro-Dent was scurrying into the kitchen, where their mother was baking. "Oh, no!" Dexter gasped. He followed Ro-Dent into the kitchen, motioning to Dee Dee. She nodded in understanding and quietly herded Ro-Dent back into the hallway as Dexter distracted their mother.

34

"Why hello Mother what are you baking hmmm sure smells good I hope you
make a lot of whatever it is be-
cause I am really hungry
thanks okay bye!" And he
ran out.

Mom looked up,
blinked, and smiled.
"Okay, hon!" she called
after him.

Dexter met his sister at the
foot of the stairs. "Whew! That
was close. Thank you for —" He
stopped short when he spotted
Ro-Dent scampering into the living room. "After him!"

In the living room, they found Ro-Dent
about to nibble on their father's favorite

35

bowling gloves. "Noooooo!" Dexter cried, tackling the mouse.

But it's hard to tackle something as small as a mouse. Ro-Dent easily slipped out of Dexter's grasp, dragging the bowling gloves with him. Just as he reached the door, Dad stepped in — and without knowing it, stepped right on the gloves. Ro-Dent kept on running, leaving the gloves behind.

Dexter scrambled to his feet. "Uh — hi, Dad!"

"Hi, son," said his father cheerfully. "Hi, Dee Dee. Say, kids, have you seen my lucky bowling gloves anywhere around? Big tournament at the Bowl-O-Rama today, y'know."

Dexter pointed at the floor. His father

looked down. "Well, what do you know? They were underfoot all along!" He picked up his gloves, chuck-ling to himself. "Boy, that's some coincidence, isn't it? Thanks, kids." And he left, whistling merrily.

Dexter and Dee Dee looked at each other and sighed with relief. Then Dee Dee pointed out into the hallway. "There he is!"

Ro-Dent was hopping cheer-fully up the stairs, hooking a left at the top. "He's heading for your bedroom," Dexter told his sister.

They burst into Dee Dee's bedroom. Ro-Dent was on

the bed, about to nibble on one of Dee Dee's favorite stuffed animals, a stuffed pink pony. Dee Dee's eyes almost popped out of her head. "Don't you dare —" she began, but it was too late. Ro-Dent took a bite.

In two seconds flat, he had eaten the entire stuffed animal.

Dee Dee stood still and silent. It was as

if she was in shock. Dexter wondered what to do. His sister loved her stuffed animals more than anything else in the world. Why, he had no idea, but he knew it was true. "It . . . it was just a pony," he said, trying to make her feel better. "I mean, you have, what, maybe eleven other stuffed . . . ponies . . . ?"

It was the *wrong* thing to say. Dee Dee's eyes turned red. Dexter gulped and stepped slowly away from her. He had never seen Dee Dee get this mad be-  fore. She was really steamed. And when Dee Dee got like this, nobody escaped alive.

Dee Dee balled her fists.

Dexter cringed.

Dee Dee began to tremble.

Dexter dived for cover behind the bed.

Finally she spoke, her voice low and cold.

"That! Mouse! Is! *HISTORY!!*"

Chapter 5

Dexter rushed after his sister. She was hauling the vacuum cleaner downstairs, her mouth set in a grim frown. "Calm yourself, Dee Dee," Dexter pleaded. "Think about what you are doing!"

"I know exactly what I'm doing!" Dee Dee growled. She plugged in the vacuum cleaner and waved the hose around. "Okay, where is he?" She spied Ro-Dent in

the corner. "Aha! There you are!" She turned on the vacuum cleaner and lunged at him.

Dexter followed his sister back and  forth across the room as she chased the mouse, trying to suck him up. "This is not the answer!" he panted. "Ro-Dent's behavior is a product of my experiments and —"

WHAM!

Dexter had run right into his father. "Whoa there, tiger," said Dad. "What's going on in here? Sounds like you two are running a race."

"Uh . . . uh . . ." Dexter twiddled his

fingers nervously. "Uh . . . Dee Dee offered to clean the living room for Mom."

Dad smiled at Dee Dee, who was still charging around the room with the vacuum. "Dee Dee," he said, "what a sweet thing to do."

Dee Dee didn't hear him. She growled

at Ro-Dent instead. But Dad thought she'd spoken to him. "What was that, hon?"

"She said thank you, Father dear," Dexter said helpfully.

"Oh." Dad smiled. "You're welcome, Dee Dee." He headed back to the garage.

Dexter wiped his brow. This was getting complicated! Worse, Ro-Dent had taken to higher ground and was now leaping from bookcase to bookcase. Dee Dee threw down the vacuum cleaner and snatched up a big butterfly net. "Oh, no you don't!" she cried, leaping after him.

Mom entered the living room and gasped. "Dee Dee, what on earth are you doing?"

When Dee Dee didn't answer, Dexter said, "Uh . . . uh . . . she is practicing a

44

new ballet exercise. It's called, um . . . Leap Net! Very good for coordination and stamina."

"Oh." Mom blinked. "Well, I just wanted to give you kids this." She handed Dexter a plate of cookies hot from the oven. "Enjoy." She headed back to the kitchen.

"Ah, much needed nourishment!" Dexter said, breathing in the sweet smell of

fresh-baked cookies. He was about to have his first one when Ro-Dent leaped down from a bookcase onto the plate. In less than three seconds, the mouse ate every cookie *and* the plate. Then he darted away.

Stunned, Dexter turned to Dee Dee. She was still now, staring at Dexter's empty hands. "The situation is worse than I ever could have imagined," Dexter told her. "Ro-Dent's appetite has become too much to control. He can never be a proper Dust Muncher now. If he isn't stopped, he will eat the entire *house*! I must stop him before it is too late!"

Dee Dee just stared at him. "You can do as you wish, Dexter. But my mission remains clear!" She gathered up the net and vacuum cleaner and rushed after Ro-Dent.

Chapter 6

Dexter paced back and forth across his lab, trying to solve the Ro-Dent problem. "If I cannot control Ro-Dent anymore, I must invent something that *can*!" he muttered. "But what could that be? What what *what*?" He suddenly stopped. At last, it had come to him. A wide grin spread across Dexter's face.

He'd had an idea.

By dawn, Dexter's latest invention was complete. "I am a genius!" he cackled gleefully.

Using his Pest Detector, Dexter located Ro-Dent up in the living room. He hurried there, carrying his invention with him, and found Dee Dee sprawled on the floor, still fully dressed, sound asleep. The

vacuum cleaner and the butterfly net lay
nearby.

Dexter gently shook his sister awake.

"Wha . . . ?" she asked, sitting up,
drooling. "Gee, I guess I forgot to go to
bed."

"Do not worry about that now," said
Dexter. "I have invented a solution to the
Ro-Dent problem."

Dee Dee's eyes flashed. "Ro-Dent! Oooo, I'm gonna get that mouse —"

"No, Dee Dee," said Dexter firmly, setting his invention on the floor. *"You* will not get him — but *Ro-Dawn* will!"

Dee Dee gawked at the little female robot mouse scampering on the floor by her feet. Ro-Dawn was made of shiny, pink metal, with big black eyes and a little purple bow at the end of

her tail. "Oh, Dexter, she's so cuuuute!" cooed Dee Dee.

"Yes, well," Dexter said in disgust, "let us hope that Ro-Dent thinks so. My Pest Detector indicates that he is asleep behind those books." He pushed a button on the Pest Detector, and it shot a beam of energy from its antenna. The beam ricocheted off the books in the bookcase, waking Ro-Dent. He leaped to the floor, landing right in front of Ro-Dawn. He stared at her in wonder.

Ro-Dawn batted her eyes at him and smiled. Ro-Dent's eyes grew big and his

jaw went slack. With a stupid mouse grin, he waved a paw at her and giggled.

"Love at first sight," Dexter noted with satisfaction. He handed Ro-Dent a tiny bulging suitcase. "Now, Ro-Dawn, follow your programming and vamoose!"

Ro-Dent took the suitcase in one paw and followed Ro-Dawn. Both mice happily scampered out the window.

Dexter dusted off his hands. "Once again, Science has saved the world."

Dee Dee put her hands on her hips. "Are you kidding? You and your Science *caused* the whole problem! And what about my stuffed pony, huh?"

Dexter had forgotten about that. And as silly as Dee Dee's stuffed animals were, he had to admit she had a right to be up-

set. Ro-Dent had destroyed one of her fa-
vorites. "I am sincerely sorry about that,
Dee Dee," he said. "I will invent a new toy
for you to replace it, okay?"

Dee Dee gave Dexter a big hug, squeez-
ing him so hard he couldn't breathe.
"Ohhhh, Dexter, thank you! You're just
the *best* baby brother ever, even if you
are a big science geek!"

Dexter wriggled out of her girlish grasp. "Yeah yeah, whatever. Now, if you will excuse me, I have work to do."

Back in his beloved laboratory, Dexter finally relaxed. "That was a close call," he said to himself, "but at least it is over. Now I can get back to work!" He sat down at his worktable and picked up a screw-

driver. He had to think of a new toy he could make for Dee Dee before she started to pester him. But first, he began to repair the damage Ro-Dent had caused.

And that's when he saw the *ants* . . .

WIN A LAB SET!

Enter *Dexter's Laboratory Super Science Challenge* and you could win one of 25 Dexter's Alien Autopsy or Dexter's Drink Laboratory lab sets (Est. Ret. Val. $19.99). See sweepstakes rules below.

Name: _____

Address: _____

City: _____ State: _____ Zip: _____

Phone: _____ Birthdate: _____

Name three things you might find in Dexter's Lab_____

_____

OFFICIAL RULES (available upon request)

NO PURCHASE NECESSARY. To enter fill out the coupon above or print your name, complete address (including city, state, and zip code), home phone number, birthdate and three things you might find in Dexter's Lab on a postcard or a 3-inch-by-5-inch card or sheet of paper, and mail it to *Dexter's Laboratory Super Science Challenge*, Trade Marketing, 557 Broadway, New York, NY 10012-3999. All entries must be received by January 31, 2003. All winners will be selected by a random drawing. Winners will be notified by February 7, 2003. Scholastic is not responsible for late, lost, stolen, misdirected, damaged, mutilated, postage due, incomplete or illegible entries or mail.

Sweepstakes is open to residents of the United States who are 12 years old or younger as of December 31, 2002. Employees, and members of their families living in the same household, of Scholastic Inc., its parent, subsidiaries, brokers, distributors, dealers, retailers, affiliates, and their respective advertising, promotion and production agencies, are not eligible to enter. Void where prohibited by law. One entry per person. Winners' first names, states and ages may be posted on www.scholastic.com/games. Twenty-five (25) winners will receive a Dexter's Alien Autopsy or Dexter's Drink Laboratory lab set (estimated retail value of $19.99). Odds of winning depend on number of entries. All prizes will be awarded. All entrants, as a condition of entry, agree to release Scholastic Inc., its affiliates, subsidiaries, distributors and agencies from any and all liability for injuries or damages of any kind sustained through participation in this sweepstakes and/or use of a prize once accepted.

No cash substitutions, transfers or assignments of prizes allowed, except by Scholastic in case of unavailability, in which case a prize of equal or greater value will be awarded.

Each winner will be required to sign and return an affidavit of eligibility and liability/publicity release within fifteen (15) days of notification attempt or an alternate winner may be selected. By accepting the prize, each winner grants to Scholastic the right to use his or her name, likeness, hometown, biographical information, and entry for purposes of advertising and promotion without further notice or compensation, except where prohibited by law. Taxes on prizes are the sole responsibility of the prize winners and their families.

For the names of the prize winners (available after February 7, 2003), send a self-addressed stamped envelope to: *Dexter's Laboratory Super Science Challenge Winner's List*, Trade Marketing, 557 Broadway, New York, NY 10012-3999.

Sponsor: Scholastic Inc., 557 Broadway, New York, NY 10012

SCHOLASTIC